The Skeleton Count

The Skeleton Count

Or, The Vampire Mistress

Elizabeth Caroline Grey

MINT EDITIONS

The Skeleton Count: Or, The Vampire Mistress was first published in 1828.

This edition published by Mint Editions 2021.

ISBN 9781513299525 | E-ISBN 9781513223889

Published by Mint Editions®

 MINT
EDITIONS

minteditionbooks.com

Publishing Director: Jennifer Newens
Design & Production: Rachel Lopez Metzger
Project Manager: Micaela Clark
Typesetting: Westchester Publishing Services

Count Rodolph, after his impious compact with the prince of darkness, ceased to study alchemy or to search after the elixir of life, for not only was a long lease of life assured him by the demon, but the same authority had declared such pursuits to be vain and delusive. But he still dabbled in the occult sciences of magic and astrology, and frequently passed day after day in fruitless speculation, concerning the origin of matter, and the nature of the soul. He studied the writings of Aristotle, Pliny, Lucretius, Josephus, Iamblicus, Sprenger, Cardan, and the learned Michael Psellus; yet was he as far as ever from attaining a correct knowledge of the things he sought to unveil from the mystery which must ever envelope them. The reveries of the ancient philosophers, of the Gnostics and the Pneaumatologists, only served to plunge him into deeper doubt, and at length he determined to pass from speculation to experiment, and put his half-formed theories to the test of practice.

After keen study of the anatomy of the human frame, and many operations and experiments on the corpse of a malefactor who had been hanged for a robbery and murder, and which he stole from the gibbet in the dead of night, and conveyed to Ravensburg Castle, with the assistance of two wretches whom he had picked up at an obscure hostelry in the town of Heidelberg, he resolved to exhume the corpse of someone recently dead, and attempt its reanimation. The formula of the necromancers for raising the dead did not suffice for their restoration to life, but only for a temporary revivification; but in an old Greek manuscript, which he found in the library of the castle, was an account of how this restored animation might be sustained by means of a miraculous liquid, for the distillation of which a recipe was given.

Count Rodolph gathered the herbs at midnight, which the Greek manuscript prescribed and distilled from them a clear gold-coloured liquid of very little taste, but most fragrant odour, which he preserved in a phial. Having discovered that a peasant's daughter, a girl of singular beauty, and about sixteen years of age, had died suddenly, and was to be buried on the day following that on which he had prepared his marvelous restorative, he set out on that day to Heidelberg to obtain the assistance of the fellows who had aided him in removing the corpse of the malefactor from the gibbet, and then returned to Ravensburg Castle, to prepare for his strange experiment.

At the solemn hour of midnight he departed secretly from the castle by a door in the eastern tower, of which he retained the key in his own possession, and bent his step to the church-yard of the neighbouring village. It was a fine moonlight night, but all the rustic inhabitants were in the arms of Morpheus, the leaden-eyed god of sleep, and the violator of the sanctity of the grave gained the church-yard unperceived. He found his hired associates waiting for him in the shadow of the wall, which was easily scaled, and being provided with shovels and a sack to contain the corpse, they set to work immediately. The fresh broken earth was soon thrown off from the lid of the coffin, which the resurrectionists removed with a screw-driver, and then the dead was disclosed to their view.

The corpse of the young maiden was lifted from its narrow resting place, and raised in the arms of the ungodly wretches whom Rodolph had hired, who deposited the inanimate clay on the margin of the grave, which they hastily filled up, and then proceeded to enclose in the sack the lifeless remains of the beautiful peasant girl. Having removed every trace of the sacrilegious theft which they had committed, one of them took the sack on his shoulders, and when he was tired his comrade relieved him, and in this manner they reached the castle. Count Rodolph led the way up the narrow stairs which led to his study chamber in the eastern turret, and having deposited the corpse upon the floor, and received their stipulated reward, the two resurrectionists were glad to make a speedy exit from a place which popular rumour began to associate with deeds of darkness and horror.

Having lighted a spirit lamp, which cast a livid and flickering light upon the many strange and mysterious objects which that chamber contained, and made the pale countenance of the corpse appear more ghastly and horrible, Count Rodolph proceeded to denude the body of its grave-clothes, which he carefully concealed, lest the sight of them, when the young maiden returned to life might strike her with a sudden horror which might prove fatal to the complete success of his daring experiment. He then placed the corpse in the centre of a magic circle which he had previously drawn upon the floor of the study, and covered it with a sheet. He had purchased some ready-made female apparel in the town of Heidelberg, and these he placed on the table in readiness for the use of the young girl, whom he felt sanguine of resuscitating.

Bertha had been, as was evidenced by her stark and cold remains, a maiden of surpassing symmetry of form and loveliness of countenance; no painter or sculptor could have desired a finer study, no poet a more inspiring theme. As she lay stretched out upon the floor of the study she looked like some beautiful carving in alabaster, or rather like a waxen figure of most artistical contrivance. Her long black hair was shaded with a purple gloss like the plumage of the raven, and her features were of most exquisite proportion and arrangement. But now her angelic countenance was livid with the pallid hue of death, the iron impress of whose icy hand was visible in every lineament.

Count Rodolph then took in his hand a magic wand, one end of which he placed on the breast of the corpse, and then proceeded to recite the cabalistic words by which necromancers call to life the slumbering tenants of the grave. When he had concluded the impious formula, an awful silence reigned in the turret, and he perceived the sheet gently agitated by the quivering of the limbs, which betokened returning animation. Then a shudder pervaded his frame in spite of himself, as he perceived the eyes of the corpse slowly open, and the dark dilated pupils fix their gaze on him with a strange and stolid glare.

Then the limbs moved, at first convulsively, but soon with a stronger and more natural motion, and then the young girl raised herself to a sitting posture on the floor of the study, and stared about her in a wild and strange manner, which made Rodolph fear that the object of his experiment would prove a wretched idiot or a raving lunatic.

But suddenly he bethought him of the restorative cordial, and snatching the phial from a shelf, he poured down the throat of the resuscitated maiden a considerable portion of the fragrant gold colored fluid which it contained. Then a ray of that glorious intellect which allies man to the angels seemed to be infused into her mind, and beamed from her dark and lustrous eyes, which rested with a soft and tender expression on the handsome countenance of the young count. Her snowy bosom, from which the sheet had fallen when she rose from her recumbent position on the floor, heaved with the returning warmth of renewed life, and the Count of Ravensburg gazed upon her with mingled sensations of wonder and delight.

As the current of life was restored, and rushed along her veins with tingling warmth, the conscious blush of instinctive modesty mantled on her countenance, and drawing the sheet over her bosom, she rose to her feet, with her long black hair hanging about her shoulders, and her dark eyes cast upon the floor. Count Rodolph then directed her attention to the clothing which he had provided, so sanguine of complete success had the daring experimentalist been, and then he withdrew from the study while the lovely object of his scientific care attired herself.

When the Count of Ravensburg returned to his study, Bertha was sitting before the fire, attired in the garments he had provided for her, and he thought that he had never beheld a more lovely specimen of her sex. She rose when he entered, and kissed his hand, as though he were a superior being, and would have remained standing, with head bowed upon her bosom, as if in the presence of a being of another world, had he not gently forced her to resume the seat from which she had risen, and inquired tenderly the state of her feelings upon a return to life so strange and wonderful. But he found that she retained no remembrance of a previous existence, and all her feelings were new and strange, like those of Eve on bursting into conscious life and being from the hand of the Omnipotent. In her mysterious passage from life to death, and from death to new life, she had lost all her previous ideas and convictions, all her experience of the past, all that she had ever acquired of knowledge; and had become a child of nature, simple and unsophisticated as a denizen of the woods, with all the keen perceptions and untrained instincts of the untutored savage.

The young girl had braided up her flowing tresses of glossy blackness, and on her cheeks dwelt color that might test a painter's skill, so rich yet delicate its hue, like the rosette tinge of some rare exotic shell, or that which a rose would cast upon an alabaster column. The young count felt himself irresistibly attracted towards the maiden, whom his science had endued with such a mysterious and preternatural existence, and she, on her part, regarded the handsome Rodolph with the wild, yet tender passion of frail humanity, mingled with the gratitude and devotion which she deemed due to one who stood to her in the position of her creator.

Thus the feelings which had so rapidly sprung up in her heart towards the only being of whom she had any conception, partook of a nature of a religious idolatry, but mingled with the grosser feelings of earth, like those which agitated in the bosom of the vestal whose sons founded Rome, or the virgin of Shen-si who was chosen from among all the women of the celestial empire to become the mother of the incarnate Foh.

"Thou art gloriously beautiful, my Bertha!" exclaimed the enamored count, pressing her in his arms. "Say that thou wilt be mine, and make me thy happy slave; thou should'st be loving as thou art lovable, beautiful child of mystery!"

"Love thee!" returned Bertha, a soft and tender expression dwelling in the clear depths of her dark eyes. "I adore thee, my creator; my soul bows itself before thee, yet my heart leaps at thy glance, though I fear it is presumptuous for the work of thy hands to look on thee with eyes of love."

"Sweet, ingenuous creature!" cried the Count of Ravensburg, kissing her coral lips and glowing cheeks. "It is I who should worship thee! Thou art mine, Bertha, now and forever. Henceforth I live only in thy smile!"

"Forever! Shall I remain with thee forever? Oh, joy incomparable! My heart's idol, I adore thee!" and the beautiful Bertha wound her white arms about his neck, and pressed her lips to his, for in the new existence which she now enjoyed her feelings knew no restraint, and she yielded to every impulse of her ardent nature.

"Come, my Bertha," said the enraptured Rodolph, "this solitary turret must not be thy world; come with me, thy Rodolph, and be the mistress of Ravensburg Castle, as thou art already of its owner's heart."

Passing his arm around the taper waist of the mysterious maiden, Rodolph took up the lamp, and quitting the eastern turret, they proceeded with noiseless steps to his chamber, where the first faint blush of day witnessed the consummation of their desires, nor did the torch of Hymen burn less brightly because no priest blessed their nuptial couch.

The presence in Ravensburg Castle of this young girl, which Rodolph, with that contempt for the opinion of the world which usually marked his actions, took no pains to conceal, became the engrossing topic of conversation in the servants' hall throughout the day, and as Rodolph had never before indulged in any intrigue, either with the peasant girls of the neighbouring village or the courtesans of Heidelburg, the circumstance seemed the more remarkable. But the beautiful Bertha seemed quite unconscious of the equivocal nature of her position in reference to the young count, and though her views of human nature became every moment more enlarged with the sphere of her existence, she still regarded Rodolph as a being of superior mold.

When night again drew his sable mantle over the sleeping earth, Rodolph and the mysterious Bertha sought their couch, and never had shone the inconstant moon on a pair so well matched as regarded physical beauty, or we may add as regarded their strange destiny—one gifted with almost superhuman powers of mind, yet in a few days to undergo so horrible a transformation, and far removed by that strange fate from ordinary mortals; the other endowed with such singular beauty yet doomed to the dreadful existence of one who had passed the boundaries of the grave, and returned to life!

With sonorous and solemn stroke the bell of the castle clock proclaimed the hour of midnight, and then Bertha slowly raised herself from her lover's body and slipping from the bed, attired herself in a half-unconscious state, and stole noiselessly from the room.

Her cheeks were pale, and her eyes had the wild and stolid glare which Rodolph had observed when she awakened from the slumber of the grave; she quitted the castle, and after gazing around her, as if uncertain which way to go, she proceeded towards the village.

She stopped opposite the nearest cottage, and then advanced to the window, and shook the shutters; the fastenings being insecure, they opened with little trouble, and a broken pane of glass enabled Bertha to introduce her hand, and remove the fastenings of the window. Then she cautiously opened the window, and entered the room—she ascended the stairs on tiptoe, and entered a chamber where a little girl was in bed and fast asleep. For a moment she shuddered violently, as if struggling to repress the horrible inclination which is the dread condition of a return to life after passing the portals of death, and then she bent her face down to the child's throat, her hot breath fanned its cheek, and the next moment her teeth punctured its tender skin, and she began to suck its blood to sustain her unnatural existence!

For such is the horrible destiny of the vampire race, of whom we have yet further mysteries and secrets to unfold; and such a being was she whom Count Rodolph had taken from the grave to his bed!

Presently the child awoke with a fearful scream, and its father, leaping from his bed in the next room, hurried to her succor, but Bertha rushed past him in the dark, and escaped from the house. The peasant found the little girl much frightened, and bleeding at the throat; but she had suffered no vital injury, and having ascertained this fact, he snatched up his match-lock, and hurried after the aggressor.

"A vampire!" exclaimed the peasant, turning pale with horror, as he distinctly saw, by the light of the moon, a young female hurrying from the village at a rapid pace.

The man gave chase to the flying Bertha, and gradually gaining ground, came within gun shot, just as she reached the shelving banks of the river, when he raised his weapon to his shoulder, and fired. The report echoed along the banks of the Rhine, and Bertha screamed as the ball penetrated her back, and tumbled headlong into the stream.

ELIZABETH CAROLINE GREY

The peasant hastened back to the village, satisfied that the horrible creature was no more, and the corpse of the vampire floated on the surface of the moonlit river.

The moon was that night at the full, and shed a flood of pearly light over the picturesque scenery of the Rhine, which, throughout its whole course, is a panorama of scenic beauty, every bend revealing some object interesting either for its historical reminiscences or legendary associations. There was the village, but now the scene of a horrible outrage—the castle, thrown into alternate light and shadow by the passing of the light fleecy clouds over the face of the moon—the town of Heidelberg, sloping from the Castle of the Palatine, and spanning the river with its noble bridge—and the Rhine, here shaded by the dark rocks which overhung the opposite bank, and there reflecting the silver light of the moon. The corpse of the vampire floated down the stream for some distance, and then it became arrested in its course by the bending of the river, and lay partly out of the water on the shelving bank.

And now commenced another scene of strange and startling interest—another phase in the fearful existence of the vampire bride! For as the beams of the full moon fell on the inanimate form of that being of mystery and fear, sensation seemed slowly to return, as when the magic spells of the Count of Ravensburg resuscitated her from the grave; her eyes opened, her bosom rose and fell with the warm pulsations of returning life; her limbs moved spasmodically, and then she rose from the bank, and shuddering at the recollection of what had occurred to her, she wrung the water from her saturated garments, and ran towards the castle at a pace accelerated by fear.

Having admitted herself into the castle, she sought the count's chamber with noiseless steps, and having taken off and concealed her wet clothes, she returned to his bed without his being aware that she had ever quitted it. The count was surprised to find that his mistress took no refreshment throughout the day, but he was led to consider it as one of the natural laws of her strange existence, and thought no more about it.

But in the village, the utmost excitement prevailed when it became known that the cottage of Herman Klans had been visited by a vampire during the night, and his little daughter bitten by the horrible creature. All day long the cottage of the mysterious visitation was beset by the wondering villagers, who crossed themselves piously, and wondered who the vampire could have been, and the services of the priest were called into requisition to prevent the little blue-eyed Minna becoming a vampire after death, as is supposed to be the case with those who have the misfortune to be bitten by one of those horrible creatures, just as a person becomes mad after the bite of a mad dog or cat.

According to the terms of the compact which had been entered into between Count Rodolph and the demon, its conditions did not come into operation until seven days after the signing of the dreadful bond, and as day after day flew on, Rodolph dreaded the necessity of acquainting Bertha with the terrible transformation which he must nightly undergo. But he knew how impossible it would be to keep his hideous and appalling metamorphosis a secret from his mistress, and he reflected that if he made her the confidant of his terrible fate it would be the more likely to remain unknown to the rest of the world. He accordingly nerved his mind to the appalling revelation which he had to make, and on the seventh day after his compact with Lucifer, he disclosed to her his awful secret.

"Bertha," said he, in a sad and solemn tone, "I am about to entrust thee with a terrible secret; swear to me that thou wilt never divulge it."

"I swear," she replied.

"Know, then," continued the count, lowering his voice to a hoarse whisper, "that, by virtue of a compact with the infernal powers of evil and of darkness, I am endowed with a term of life and youth amounting almost to the boon of immortality but to this inestimable gift, there is a condition attached which commences this night, and which I almost tremble to impart to thee."

"Fear not, my Rodolph!" exclaimed his beautiful mistress, twining her round white arms about his neck, "thy Bertha can never love thee less, and her soul the rather clings to thee more intensely for the preternatural gift which links thy destiny more closely to my own. For mine, too, is a strange and fearful existence, which I owe to thee, and therefore shall I cling to thee the more fondly for the kindred doom which allies us to each other while it lifts us far above ordinary mortals."

"Then prepare thy ears for a dread revelation, Bertha," returned the Count of Ravensburg. "Each night of my future existence, at the hour of sunset, my doom divests me of my mortal shape, and I become a skeleton until sunrise on the morn ensuing. Now, thou knowest all, my Bertha, and be it thy care to prevent the dreadful secret from becoming known."

"It shall, my brave Rodolph!" exclaimed Bertha, her eyes glittering with a strange expression, as she thought of the facility which her lover's strange doom would allow for her nocturnal absences from the castle. "No eye but mine shall witness thy transformation, and I will watch over thee until thy return to thy natural shape."

"Thanks, my Bertha!" returned Rodolph, embracing her. "The hour draws nigh when I must relinquish for the night my mortal form; come, love, to our chamber, and see that no prying eye beholds the ghastly change."

Bertha and her lover accordingly repaired to their chamber, and when the luminary of day sank below the horizon, leaving the traces of his splendor on the western sky, the Count Rodolph shrunk to a grisly skeleton, and fell upon the bed. Bertha shuddered as she witnessed the horrid transformation, and they lay down on the bed until midnight, the necessity of secrecy overcoming any repugnance she might otherwise have felt to the horrible contiguity of the skeleton, but when the castle clock proclaimed the hour of midnight with iron tongue, she rose from the bed, and locking the door of the chamber which contained so strange a guest, she stole from the castle to sate her unnatural appetite for human blood.

The moon rode high in the heavens on that night of unfathomable mystery and horror, and her silver beams shone through the chamber-window of Theresa Delmar, one of the loveliest maidens in the village of Ravensburg, revealing a snowy neck, and a white and dimpled shoulder, shaded by the bright golden locks which strayed over the pillow. The maiden's blue eyes were concealed by their thin lids and their long silken fringes, and her snowy bosom gently rose and fell beneath the white coverlet as the thoughts which agitated her by day, mingled in her dreams at night. Silence reigned in the thatched cottage, and throughout the village was only occasionally broken by the barking of some watchful house-dog.

But soon after midnight the silence was broken by a slight noise at the chamber window as if someone was endeavoring to obtain an entrance, and the flood of moonlight which streamed upon the maiden's bed was obscured by the form of a woman standing on the windowsill. Still Theresa slumbered on, nor dreamed of peril so near, for the woman had succeeded in opening the window, and in another moment she stood within the room.

With slow and cautious step she softly approached the bed whereon the maiden reposed so calmly, little dreaming how dread a visitant was near her couch, and then she shuddered involuntarily as she bent over the sleeping girl, and her long dark ringlets mingled with the masses of golden hair which shaded the white shoulder, and the partially exposed bosom of Theresa Delmar. Her lips touched the young girl's neck, her sharp teeth punctured the white skin, and then she began to suck greedily, quaffing the vital fluid which flowed warm and quick in the maiden's veins, and sapping her life to maintain her own!

Still Theresa awoke not, for the puncture made in her throat by the teeth of the horrible creature was little larger than that which would be made by a leech, and the vampire sucked long and greedily, for her long abstinence from blood had sharpened her unnatural appetite. Suddenly Theresa awoke with a start, doubtless caused by some unpleasant transition in her dreams, but she did not immediately cry out, for she felt no pain, and as yet she was scarcely conscious of her danger. But in a few seconds she was thoroughly awake, and her surprise and horror may be more easily imagined than described, when she found bending over her, and sucking her blood, the horrible creature that had but a few nights previously attacked Minna Klaus, and which the child's father thought he had destroyed.

Spell-bound by the glittering eyes of the vampire, she lay without the power to scream, until the appalling horror of her situation became too great for endurance, her quivering nerves were strung to their utmost power of extension, and a wild shriek burst from her lips. Even then the horrible creature did not leave its hold, but continued to suck from her palpitating veins the crimson current of her life, until footsteps were heard hastily approaching the chamber, and the lovely Theresa, whose screams seemed to have broken the fascination which had bound her in its thrall, struggled so violently that Bertha was compelled to relinquish her horrid banquet. Springing to the window, she effected her escape, just as heavy blows resounded on the door of the chamber, and her affrighted victim sank insensible on the bed.

"What is the matter, Theresa? Open the door!" exclaimed her terrified parents; but they received no answer.

Then Delmar broke open the door, and he and his wife rushed into the room and found their daughter lying insensible on the bed, with spots of blood on her throat and bosom, and the window wide open.

"The vampire has come to life again, and has attacked our Theresa!" exclaimed her mother. "See the blood-marks on her dear neck! Raise the village, Delmar, to pursue the monster."

"Oh, dear! where am I? Has it gone, mother?" inquired Theresa, as she recovered from her swoon, and gazed in a frightened manner round the room.

"Yes, it has gone now, dear," said her mother. "What was it like?"

"Aye, what was it like?" added old Delmar. "Perhaps it was not the same one that neighbor Klans shot at the other night."

"Oh, yes! it was a young woman, and as much like Bertha Kurtel as ever one pea was like another," replied the young girl, shuddering.

"Holy virgin!" exclaimed her mother, crossing herself with a shudder. "Bertha Kurtel a vampire, and returned from the grave to prey upon our Theresea! Oh, horrible!"

Delmar hurriedly dressed himself, and catching up an axe, he hastened to call up Klans and others to pursue the vampire, and in a few minutes the whole village was in commotion. About twenty men armed themselves with whatever weapon came first to hand, and followed the direction which the vampire had taken when chased by Herman Klans on a former occasion. They searched every bush all round the village, to which they returned at sunrise without having found any trace of the object of their search. Delmar found his daughter somewhat faint from fright and loss of blood, but not otherwise injured by the vampire's attack. The greatest excitement prevailed in that usually quiet village, and all the morning, groups of men stood about the little street, or clustered round Delmar's cottage, conversing in low and mysterious whispers of the dreadful visitation which the village had a second time received.

"What a shocking thing it would be if a pretty girl like Theresa Delmar was to become a vampire when she dies," observed one. "And who knows what may happen now she has been bitten by one of those horrible creatures?"

"And poor little Minna Klaus," said another.

"Ah, and we do not know how long the list may be if we do not put a stop to it," added one of the rustic group. "I have heard Father Ambrose say that they generally attack females and children."

"Who can it be? that is what I want to know," said old Klaus. "Why, Theresa declares it was just like Bertha Kurtel," returned another, shaking his voice to a whisper.

"Bertha Kurtel!" repeated a youth who had loved her who once bore that name. "Bertha a vampire! impossible."

"It is easily ascertained," observed the gruff voice of the village blacksmith. "We have only to take up the coffin and see if she is in it, as she ought to be. If we do not find her we shall know what's o'clock."

"If it was not for her parents' feelings I really should like to be satisfied whether it is Bertha," remarked old Delmar.

"Feelings!" repeated the smith, in a surly tone. "Have we not all got our feelings? Are we to have our wives and children attacked in this manner, and all turned into vampires, and let other people's fine feelings prevent us from having satisfaction for it?"

"There is something in that," observed Delmar, scratching his head with an air of perplexity.

"I would make one if anybody else would go," said Herman Klaus, after a pause.

"And I will be another," exclaimed the smith, looking around him. "Now who will go and have a peep in the churchyard to see whose coffin is empty?"

Several expressed themselves ready, and others following their example the smith proceeded to the churchyard, backed by about twenty of the most resolute of the villagers, to reenact the scene which had taken place there but a few nights since. On arriving at the churchyard the smith and another immediately set to work to throw the earth out of the grave, which was soon accomplished, and amid the most breathless silence the smith proceeded to remove the lid of the coffin.

"Look here, neighbors," said he, turning pale in spite of himself. "The lid has been removed, and the coffin is empty!"

"So it is!" exclaimed Herman Klaus.

"Then is it not plain that Bertha is the vampire—the horrible creature that sucked the blood of Theresa Delmar and little Minna Klans?" said the smith, looking round upon the throng which had been swelled during the work of exhumation by idlers from the village.

"But where is she now? that is the question," observed Herman Klans.

"This must be investigated," said the smith. "We must keep watch for the vampire, and catch it; then we must either burn it, or drive a stake through the creature's body, for they say those are the only methods that will effectually fix a vampire."

The wondering group of peasants returned to the village, and great was the grief of the Kurtels at the horrible discovery that their daughter had become a vampire, and the youth who had so loved Bertha in her human state became delirious on hearing the confirmation of the suspicion which Theresa's assertion had first excited. The ordinary occupations of the villagers were entirely neglected throughout the day, and nothing was talked of but vampires and werewolves, and other human transformations more terrific and appalling than any recorded in the metamorphoses of Ovid. Towards the evening the venerable seneschal of the Count of Ravensburg arrived in the village and had an interview with the Delmars, after which he visited the cottage of Herman Klans, and a vague rumor spread like wildfire from house to house, to the effect that the vampire was an inmate of Ravensburg Castle.

The communication made by the seneschal to Delmar and Klans was to the effect that, on the morning following the interment of Bertha Kurtel, a young female exactly resembling her in form, features, voice, and every individual peculiarity, had appeared in a mysterious manner at the castle, and had resided there ever since in the capacity of the count's mistress. No one knew who she was, where she came from, or how she obtained admission into the castle; and the occurrences in the village having reached the ears of the count's retainers and domestics, accompanied with the suspicion that the vampire was the revived Bertha Kurtel, the seneschal had hastened to the village to report his observations. The abstinence of the count's mistress from food was deemed corroborative of the suspicion that she was a vampire, and the seneschal's report caused the utmost excitement among the villagers. Symptoms of hostile intentions soon became visible, and in less than half an hour, more than a hundred men were proceeding in a disorderly manner towards the castle, armed with every imaginable weapon, and swearing to put an end to the vampire.

Count Rodolph and his beautiful mistress were sitting at a window which commanded a view of the road for some distance, the small white hand of Bertha locked in that of her lover, and whispering words of tenderness and love, when their attention was attracted by a disorderly mob approaching from the village.

"What can this mean?" said Rodolph, rising.

"Oh, this is what I have dreaded!" exclaimed Bertha, turning pale, and clasping her hands in a terrified manner: "your studies have caused you to be suspected of necromancy, my Rodolph, they come to attack the castle."

"I fear thou art right, dearest," said the count: "but we will give them a warm reception. Ho! a lawless mob menaces the castle with danger: make fast the gates; bar every door; bid my retainers man the battlements to repel the attack."

"And sunset is approaching," exclaimed Bertha, with a meaning glance at her lover.

"Do thou retire, sweet love, to thy chamber," said Rodolph; "fear not for me; I bear a charmed life, and neither sword nor shot will avail against it. If this lawless rabble be not dispersed when the dread moment comes all hope will be lost, and they shall behold the grisly change. Perhaps they may be struck with a sudden panic, and we may be enabled to fly into another country."

Bertha retired after embracing the count, and shut herself up in her chamber. Preparations were immediately made to resist the attack of the insurgent villagers, who continued to advance upon the castle, yelling like savages, and breathing vengeance against the vampire mistress of Count Rodolph.

"Down with the vampire!" was the hoarse and sullen cry which rolled like distant thunder from a hundred throats, and then the mob drew up before the castle gates, and the smith struck them heavily with his ponderous hammer.

The count took an arquebuse and fired at the mob, very few of whom were provided with fire-arms; one of the peasants was wounded, and with a shout of rage and defiance a volley of shot, arrows, and stones was directed against the beleaguered castle. The smith continued to batter away at the gate, aided by several stalwart fellows with axes, and though several of the mob were killed by the fire of the men-at-arms, those who were endeavoring to force the gate were protected by the overhanging battlements, and continued to ply their implements with unwearied energy.

Could Rodolph turned pale, and shuddered as he listened to the wild cries of the assailants, not from fear, for apart from his invulnerability he was inaccessible to that feeling, but from the horrible ideas engendered from these shouts, having reference to the beautiful Bertha Kurtel. Had her resuscitation from the grave endowed her with the horrible nature of the vampire? Could that lovely creature sustain her renewed existence with the blood of her former companions? Horrible! yet, had she not hinted at something of the kind when he revealed to her the horrors of his own strange doom? It must be so, then; and he shuddered violently at the appalling idea.

"Down with the vampire!" was still the menacing cry which rose from the assailants, who at length succeeded in breaking down the gates, and rushed tumultuously into the court-yard, shouting and brandishing their weapons.

Undismayed by the fire from the battlements, they commenced

ELIZABETH CAROLINE GREY

an attack on the doors and windows of the castle, and now they were all crowded in the courtyard, Count Rodolph thought the moment favorably for a sally. Drawing his sword, and commanding a score of his armed retainers to follow him, he suddenly opened a door leading into the court-yard, and fell furiously on the flank of the assailants. For a moment they were thrown into confusion, but they quickly rallied, when Count Rodolph and his little party were surrounded and compelled to act on the defensive. The ruddy beams of the setting sun were already purpling the distant hills when the peasants marched upon the castle, and as his broad disk sank below the horizon, the aspect of the Count of Ravensburg suddenly underwent a marvelous change, and much as the insurgents had wondered to see arrows glance off from his body, and their swords rebound as if their stroke fell on a giant oak, how much greater was their astonishment when they beheld him suddenly transformed into a fleshless skeleton!

"It is some devise of Satan!—he is a sorcerer!" cried the stalwart smith, brandishing his huge hammer. "Come on, mates—down with the vampire!"

"Down with the vampire!" echoed from the mob, and the count's retainers giving way on all sides, as much appalled as the peasants at this horrible metamorphosis, the assailants rushed into the castle by the open door, and marched from room to room, looking in every closet and under every bed, while the terrified Bertha flew from one apartment to another, until she at length sought refuge in the highest apartment of the eastern turret, that chamber which had witnessed her return from death to her renewed state of strange and horrible existence. She had locked and bolted the door of the study, but what availed these obstacles against a furious mob, animated by their success in gaining the castle, and bent upon destruction and revenge? The door cracked, yielded, was forced open, and several men rushed into the little chamber.

"Here she is!—here is the vampire!" cried the foremost, and despite her piercing shrieks and earnest supplications for mercy, the wretched Bertha was dragged out of the study, with her long black hair hanging in wild disorder about her shoulders, and her beautiful countenance pale with overpowering terror.

"Mercy, indeed! What mercy can we feel for a vampire?" cried the peasants, and the terrified creature was dragged down the turret stairs by one or two of the boldest, for few would venture to come in contact with the dreaded being.

As they reached the foot of the stairs a volume of smoke rolled along the passage, and the crackling of burning wood told them that some of their companions had set fire to the castle.

"Now what shall we do with the vampire?" said her remorseless captors.

"Throw her into the Rhine!" suggested one.

"Tie her up and shoot at her!" said another.

"What will be the use of that?" objected a third. "Nothing but fire or a sharp stake will destroy a vampire. Let us shut her up in the castle, and burn her to ashes!"

"Yes, yes! burn the vampire!" shouted a score of voices.

"No, no!—I say, no!" cried the smith. "Let us carry her to the churchyard, put her in her coffin again, and peg her down with a stake, so that she can never rise again."

The suggestion of the smith was approved of, and the wretched Bertha was half-dragged and half-carried, more dead than alive, towards the village church. The flames were bursting forth from all parts of the castle when the lawless spoilers left it, and a red glow hung over its ancient towers; the work of destruction was rapid, and in a few hours naught but the bare and blackened walls were left standing.

On the destroyers of Ravensburg Castle reaching the churchyard, the almost lifeless form of Bertha Kurtel was dragged to the grave, which had been left open, and flung rudely into the coffin. Then a sharp pointed stake was produced, which had been prepared by the way, and the smith plunged it with all the force of his sinewy arms into the abdomen of the doomed vampire. A piercing shriek burst from her pale lips as the horrible thrust aroused her to consciousness, and as her clothes became dabbed with the crimson stream of life, and the smith lifted his heavy hammer and drove the stake through her quivering body, the transfixed wretch writhed convulsively, and the contortions of her countenance were fearful to behold. Thus impaled in her coffin, and while her limbs yet quivered with the last throes of dissolution, the earth was replaced and rammed down by the tread of many feet.

But those strange and terrible scenes were not yet ended. A young peasant of equal curiosity and boldness, and who had been engaged in the attack upon the castle and the horrible tragedy which followed it, was anxious to know more of the strange affair of the skeleton, which had been left in the courtyard where it fell, none of the villagers caring to interfere with so ghastly an object. He therefore stole away a little before midnight, and went towards the castle, where the fire was dying out, though a fiery glow was still reflected from the moldering embers of beams and rafters. He advanced cautiously through the broken gates of the castle, and shuddered slightly as he perceived the skeleton of the Count of Ravensburg still lying on the pavement of the courtyard.

He determined to watch until daylight, and see what became of the grisly relics of mortality, which a few hours before had been the young and handsome Count of Ravensburg. The hours passed slowly on from midnight to the dawn of another day, and when the rising sun tinged the eastern sky with crimson and gold, a strange spectacle was witnessed by the solitary watcher in the court-yard of Ravensburg Castle.

The skeleton rose slowly from the pavement, and assumed the form of Count Rodolph, just as he appeared at the moment preceding his transformation on the evening before. A cold perspiration bedewed the brow of the peasant, and his hair stood erect with terror, on witnessing this sudden metamorphosis. The count looked up at the dilapidated walls and towers of his castle, and shuddered violently, and crossing the court-yard, passed through the broken gate.

The peasant then hastened to the village, and reported what he had seen, which was a source of much marvel to the rustic inhabitants. The story of the skeleton count, and his vampire mistress, quickly spread all over Germany, but the villagers were no more molested by vampires, for Bertha Kurtel was securely fixed in her coffin, and no ill effects ensued from her attacks upon Theresa Delmar and little Minna Klans.

END

A Note About the Author

Elizabeth Caroline Grey (1798–1869) was an English novelist and one of the nineteenth century's leading author of penny dreadfuls. Although her life story is unclear—some scholars believe she never existed at all, or that her name was a pseudonym used by James Malcolm Rymer— Grey is traditionally said to have been the niece of a famous actress. She married a reporter known as Colonel Grey, taught in a London girls' school, and wrote fiction in her spare time. *The Skeleton Count: Or The Vampire Mistress* (1828), her most famous novel, is notable for being the first vampire story written by a woman.

A Note from the Publisher

Spanning many genres, from non-fiction essays to literature classics to children's books and lyric poetry, Mint Edition books showcase the master works of our time in a modern new package. The text is freshly typeset, is clean and easy to read, and features a new note about the author in each volume. Many books also include exclusive new introductory material. Every book boasts a striking new cover, which makes it as appropriate for collecting as it is for gift giving. Mint Edition books are only printed when a reader orders them, so natural resources are not wasted. We're proud that our books are never manufactured in excess and exist only in the exact quantity they need to be read and enjoyed.

Discover more of your favorite classics with Bookfinity™.

- Track your reading with custom book lists.
- Get great book recommendations for your personalized Reader Type.
- Add reviews for your favorite books.
- AND MUCH MORE!

Visit **bookfinity.com** and take the fun Reader Type quiz to get started.

Enjoy our classic and modern companion pairings!